• I AM READING •

The Giant Postman

SALLY GRINDLEY

Illustrated by
WENDY SMITH

KING*f*ISHER
NEW YORK

For Postman Martin—S.G.
To R & P—W.S.

KINGFISHER
Larousse Kingfisher Chambers Inc.
95 Madison Avenue
New York, New York 10016

First published in 2000
2 4 6 8 10 9 7 5 3 1

1TR/0500/TWP/RNB/150ARM

LIBRARY OF CONGRESS CATALOGING–IN–PUBLICATION DATA
has been applied for.

ISBN 0-7534-5319-3

Printed in Singapore

Contents

Chapter One

"He's coming!" screamed a little girl.

"He's coming!" shouted the
ice cream man.

"He's coming!" shouted
the window cleaner.

Children dropped their
schoolbags and ran.

Shoppers dropped their
shopping and ran.

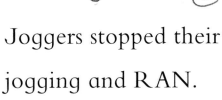

Joggers stopped their
jogging and RAN.

Soon, the street was empty.

It was so quiet you could hear a pin drop.

5

Then there was a loud thump.

And another. And another.

THUMP! THUMP! THUMP!

Great big boots cracked the

sidewalk.

Great big boots shook the houses.

Behind closed curtains, people
shivered with fear.

"Please don't have any mail for us,"
they whispered.

THUMP! THUMP! THUMP!

The Giant Postman was coming.

Chapter Two

Billy and his mom lived at Number 24.

"Get under the table!" screamed

Billy's mom.

But Billy stood at the window

and watched the Giant Postman

stomping from door to door.

THUMP! THUMP! THUMP!

The Giant Postman was right outside

Billy's house.

BANG! BANG! BANG!

He pounded on the door.

"I have a package for you,"

he bellowed.

"Just leave it outside, please," called Billy's mom. "Oh, no," replied the Giant Postman. "I don't want it to be stolen."

BANG! BANG! BANG!

Billy quickly opened the door and hid behind it.

"Here you are!" bellowed the Giant Postman, and he dropped the package on the floor.

Then he stomped off down the street.

THUMP! THUMP! THUMP!

"Has he gone?" whispered Billy's mom.

Billy peered around the door.

"Yes, he's gone," he said.

Then Billy walked out into the street.

11

The street was still empty.

Mrs. White's front gate was hanging off its hinges.

Mr. Homer's cabbages were trampled to the ground.

Mrs. Atwell's cat was on the roof of her house, quivering with fright.

One by one the villagers appeared.
"Is it safe?" they asked.

"Yes," said Billy, "he's gone.

But it's time we did something.

Getting letters is supposed to be fun."

"We're all too scared to do anything,"

they said.

"Well, I'm not," said Billy.

"I'm going to write a letter to the postman and ask him to stop frightening us."

The crowd gasped.

"And I'm going to deliver it myself!"

Chapter Three

That same day, Billy sat down and wrote his letter.

Dear Mr. Postman,
My name is Billy and I live in the village.
I am writing to ask you to please stop frightening us.

Mr. Homer is very upset about his
cabbages and Mrs. Atwell's cat
won't come down from the roof.
We would like to be friends
with you.
Best wishes,
Billy

He wrote "Mr. Postman"
on an envelope and
put the letter inside.
Then Billy set off
to the woods where
the Giant Postman lived.
"Don't go, Billy!" cried
his mom.

BY HAND
Mr. Postman
The Woods

"Don't go, Billy!" cried the villagers.

But Billy kept going,

past the bakery . . .

past the shoe store . . .

18

past the school . . .

on and on, until at last he reached

the woods.

19

The woods were very dark.

Billy heard strange noises.

CRICK! CRACK! RUSTLE!

He began to feel frightened.

CRICK!

He wanted to go back.

CRACK!

But he made himself go on.

RUSTLE!

Faster and faster he went, until . . .

21

at last he came to a clearing.

There stood the Giant Postman's

great big house.

Billy was surprised to see that

the yard was full of flowers.

He walked up to the door.

Chapter Four

TAP! TAP! TAP!

Billy knocked on the Giant

Postman's door.

Nobody came.

TAP! TAP! TAP!

He knocked a little louder.

At last, he heard footsteps—

SHUFFLE, SHUFFLE, SHUFFLE.

23

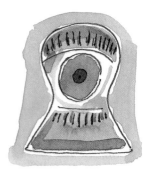 Then Billy saw a giant
eye peeping through
the keyhole.

"What do you want?"
bellowed the Giant Postman.

"I b-b-brought a letter,"
Billy stammered.

"What do you mean?" said the
Giant Postman.

"*I* deliver the letters."

"It's a letter for
you," said Billy.

Slowly, slowly
the door opened.
The Giant Postman stared
at Billy.

He took the envelope and peered at it.

Slowly, slowly he pulled out the letter.

He read it over and over again.

Billy shifted his feet nervously

on the doorstep.

He was all alone with

the Giant Postman.

Billy felt very scared.

Then he noticed that

the Giant Postman

was wearing slippers

and had holes in the

elbows of his sweater.

Billy looked at his

face and thought

he saw him smile.

But the Giant Postman turned away
and closed the door without a word.

Billy ran all the way home,

through the dark woods . . .

on and on, until at last he reached

his house.

"Oh, Billy!" cried his mom.

"Thank goodness you're safe."

"He read my letter," said Billy,

"but he didn't say a word.

I hope I haven't made him angry."

But that night Billy remembered
the yard full of flowers.
He remembered the slippers,
and the woolly sweater with holes.
The Giant Postman didn't seem
so frightening without his uniform
and his great big boots.

Chapter Five

The next morning, Billy looked

out of his window.

It wasn't long before he saw

people running to hide.

THUMP! THUMP! THUMP!

The Giant Postman was coming.

Great big boots cracked the

sidewalk.

Great big boots shook the houses.

THUMP! THUMP! THUMP!

The Giant Postman was right outside
Billy's house.

"Get under the table!" screamed
Billy's mom.

But Billy opened the window.

"Good morning, Mr. Postman," he said.

From his bag the Giant Postman pulled an
enormous envelope.

"I have a letter for you," he said.

Then he stomped off down the

empty street.

THUMP! THUMP! THUMP!

Billy ran downstairs.

His hands shook as he took the

letter out of the envelope.

He read:

Dear Billy,
Thank you for your letter. I've never gotten one before. I don't mean to frighten people. I'm sorry about Mr. Homer's cabbages. I'm afraid I'm clumsy in my boots. Will you write to me again tomorrow, please? It's my birthday.
Your friend,
Mr. Postman

Billy smiled and ran out into
the street.

"It's all right," he said, waving
the letter. "You can come out."
He danced up and down
until a crowd gathered
around him.

Then he showed them the letter.

"Never got a letter!"
said Mr. Homer.

"Poor thing,"
said Mrs. Atwell.

"He sounds a
little lonely,"
said Mr. White.

"I don't think he's scary
at all," said a little girl.
"I'm going to make him
a birthday card."

"I guess he can't help being clumsy
in his big boots," said Billy.
Then he had an idea.

Chapter Six

That night the villagers didn't sleep.
Lights burned in all the houses.
Delicious smells came from the
bakery, and loud noises came
from the shoe store—
BANG! THUMP! RRRRR!

Up and down the street,
people climbed ladders
and tied knots.

Just as dawn broke,

everything was ready.

The villagers stood by their windows

and waited. And waited.

THUMP! THUMP! THUMP!

The Giant Postman was coming.

THUMP!

THUMP!

The great big boots

stopped in their tracks.

The Giant Postman

stared.

And stared.

Banners and balloons hung from
every house and from every lamppost.
The banners read:

TO OUR POSTMAN, A VERY
HAPPY BIRTHDAY!

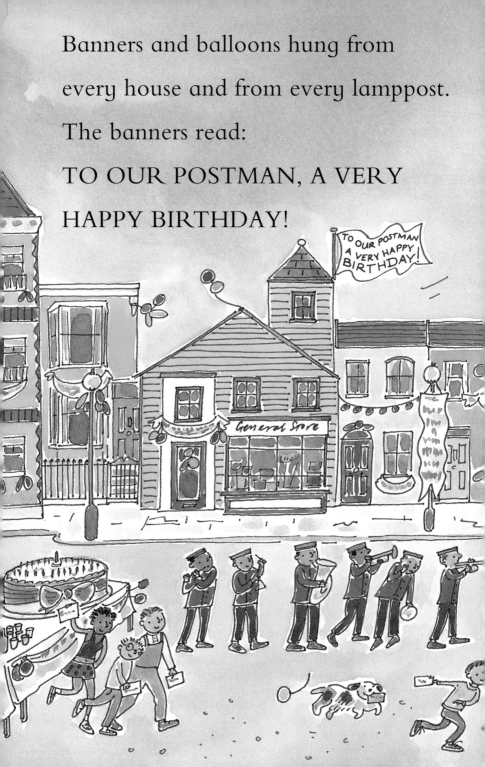

The village band began to play.

DRUM! DRUM! DRUM!

TOOT! TOOT! TOOT-TOOT!

The villagers rushed into the

street, waving birthday cards.

Billy came out of the shoe store
pulling a cart. On top of the
cart was the biggest package
you have ever seen.

"HAPPY BIRTHDAY,
MR. POSTMAN," said Billy.
"This present is from all of us."

Gently, the Giant Postman pulled off the paper and lifted the lid of the great big box.

"Just what I've always wanted!" he gasped.

The Giant Postman held up a

great big pair of new sneakers.

"Try them on!" the villagers cried.

So, he tried them on.

"They're perfect," he said.

"They're so soft and springy."

He walked up and down

without a single THUMP.

Then the Giant Postman
smiled a great big smile.
The villagers cheered.

"Time for a party," Billy yelled.

"Time for a party," everyone cried.

The Giant Postman danced down

the street.

"Time for a party!" he bellowed

with delight.

"This is the very best birthday ever!"

About the Author and Illustrator

Sally Grindley is an award-winning writer.
Her own postman is not like the clumsy
Giant Postman at all—he hates having to knock on
the door to deliver a package. "He always comes
early," says Sally, "and he knows I'm embarrassed
by my just-got-out-of-bed, crumpled-face,
tangled-hair state." Sally Grindley's other books
for Kingfisher include *What Are Friends For?*
and *What Will I Do Without You?*

Wendy Smith has written and illustrated a lot
of books for children, and also teaches art and
illustration at Brighton University. Wendy says,
"I love to hear the mail drop rattle in the morning.
I enjoy guessing who the letter is from, and
wondering what news I'm going to read!"

If you've enjoyed reading *The Giant Postman*, try these other **I Am Reading** books:

ALLIGATOR TAILS AND CROCODILE CAKES
Nicola Moon and Andy Ellis

BARN PARTY
Claire O'Brien and Tim Archbold

JJ RABBIT AND THE MONSTER
Nicola Moon and Ant Parker

JOE LION'S BIG BOOTS
Kara May and Jonathan Allen

KIT'S CASTLE
Chris Powling and Anthony Lewis

MR. COOL
Jacqueline Wilson and Stephen Lewis

MRS. HIPPO'S PIZZA PARLOR
Vivian French and Clive Scruton